EXPLORING PLANET VIDA

David Ellis Grey

To order additional copies of this book, contact:
Xlibris
844-714-8691
www.Xlibris.com
Orders@Xlibris.com

ISBN: Softcover   978-1-6698-4064-0
         EBook   978-1-6698-4063-3

Print information available on the last page

Rev. date: 07/29/2022

I dedicate this book to my children: Nicole, Karilyn, Kasey, Jessica, Bryan, Christine and Taylee who inspired me to put my fun bedtime stories in writing. And to my loving wife, Heidi who supported me in the writing of this book, and many more to come. I love you all!

The crew of the United States Space Shuttle said goodbye to their families just before they launched into outer space on a mission to the International Space Station. Their families waved one final time as the rocket lifted off the ground. The launch was a success!

While enroute to the space station, a communication satellite floating in space became unbalanced, went off course, and abruptly struck the Space Shuttle. This forced the Space Shuttle to spin out of control and unknowingly bounced into another galaxy.

The crew of the Space Shuttle soon realized they were forever lost in space. However, as the shuttle drifted for several days in space, they noticed a planet that looked very similar to Earth. From space, as they looked at this planet, they could see land and oceans. They noticed the land is connected all around this new world. The oceans are also connected together.

So they decided to enter the atmosphere of this newly discovered planet and was able to maneuver the shuttle to an open field where they could land. Unfortunately, the shuttle was damaged during touchdown and became unrepairable.

As the astronauts stepped out of the shuttle and explored the area around
their landing site, they soon realized that they could remove their helmets
and breathe the air. They looked around and noticed beautiful green hills,
and felt a warm breeze around them.

During their exploration, they discovered a city, very similar to cities on Earth, where people could live, work, go to school, shop, and play. It was almost as if they had landed back on Earth! They noticed people who looked similar to people on Earth. They noticed parents playing with their children. They also noticed many animals walking around with people, even dogs, cats, horses, cows, and sheep. They saw every kind of animal you can imagine. There was almost as many animals walking around as people.

The astronauts entered the city and were very determined to learn more about this new world.

The citizens of this new planet welcomed the crew of the Space Shuttle and are willing to share information about life on their planet.

They have electricity generated by the wind or solar energy to power their homes and businesses. Automobiles exist, but gasoline-powered engines do not. There are no natural resources in the ground, such as natural gas, oil or coal. Cars, trucks, and buses run on solar energy or wind.

This newly discovered planet also has high-speed trains powered by solar energy. Airplanes do not exist. But, because land connected to every corner of the planet, people could travel by car, high-speed train, bus, bicycle, and many other types of land transportation to go anywhere they wanted.

Cell phones and computers do not exist. In some ways it appears this newly discovered planet is behind earth in certain technology, but it seems they are well advanced over earth in many other ways.

The planet's trees stay fresh and green and never change color during the year. Their instruments indicate air temperature at 70 degrees day and night. Summer, fall, and winter seasons did not exist. The planet does not experience extreme heat or freezing cold temperatures, ever. It is like spring-time all year.

When the astronauts asked about the type of fish that live in their lakes and oceans, they are surprised to learn that fish do not exist! The fresh water from lakes and oceans are used for many things including drinking, cooking, washing, bathing and crop irrigation.

Animals on this planet live as long as humans. Unlike earth, animals are not considered a food source. Animals are respected and treated very similar to humans. Food consumption comes from grain, fruit and vegetables that is grown in their very rich soil.

There is no cancer, disease or illness of any kind. Doctors provide medical help to those who are injured.
Can this possibly be an earth-like planet where everyone can live healthy, happy and enjoy what their planet provides for them?

Being stranded in this new and different world was a challenge for the crew of the Space Shuttle. They not only had to determine how to help the people of planet VIDA discover new technology, but also learn new concepts and ideas from them that will better serve the people of planet earth. Without technology, it could take several months to devise a method to return the crew of the Space Shuttle safely to earth.

However, the knowledge and training the shuttle crew received on earth, along with knowledge obtained from the citizens of planet VIDA will allow them to build a new space vehicle made from solar powered materials that will hopefully transport the shuttle crew safely back to earth.

After several months of hard work, a new and more futuristic space vehicle is constructed! The crew said their good-byes and thanked the generous people of planet VIDA for their help and generosity.

The launch was successful as the shuttle crew made their way back home to earth.

Printed in the United States
by Baker & Taylor Publisher Services